Hi Fella

Look for these and
other Apple Paperbacks
in your local bookstore!

Orphaned Pup
by Eleanor J. Lapp

Margaret's Moves
by Berniece Rabe

The Secret Horse
by Marion Holland

Me and Katie (the Pest)
by Ann M. Martin

When the Dolls Woke
by Marjorie Filley Stover

Hi Fella

Era Zistel

Illustrated by Taylor Oughton

AN
APPLE
PAPERBACK

SCHOLASTIC INC.
New York Toronto London Auckland Sydney

ISBN 0-590-42047-X

Copyright © 1977 by Era Zistel.

12 11 10 9 8 7 6 5 4 3 2 1   11   8 9/8 0 1 2 3/9

For my lifelong friend in Sandusky
Mary McCann

1

At first the only name he had was Pup, but as he grew older the farmer gave him others. Bad Dog meant he had done something wrong, although he seldom knew what. Good Dog was just the opposite, meaning the farmer was pleased, and when he heard that name he always wagged his tail. But best of all he liked Hi Fella, because that meant the farmer was in a very good mood. Whenever he was called Hi Fella he not only wagged his tail but leaped all around the farmer, who would stop to play with him for a while.

Most of the day the farmer was away, working in the fields. But Hi Fella had other company, a brother and a sister to romp with, and a mother who let him bat her face, chew on her ears, and chase her tail. Sometimes she even started a game with him herself, bowling him over to nip at his belly, making him squeal with delight.

Life on the farm was good. He had plenty to eat. Twice a day the farmer's wife put down a plate of food near the back steps, and once in a while some bones too. At night he had a nice soft bed of hay in the barn, where he slept with his mother and brother and sister. So he had every reason to be happy and none to be unhappy, until things changed. First his brother and sister disappeared. Then his mother turned cross. Then he got mixed up with the rabbits.

One morning, just after their mother had gone for her walk in the fields, the farmer came to where they were playing near the barn. Usually whenever they saw the farmer they ran to meet him, but this time he brought along a stranger, and that made them shy. Huddled together, they stared up at the stranger while he stared down at them. Finally he said, "I'll take this one," and he carried off the sister.

Hi Fella did not miss her too much because there was still his brother to play with. But a few days later the same thing happened: the farmer brought another stranger, and the brother was taken away. That left only his mother to keep him company, and for some reason she did not seem to like him anymore. Whenever he tried to start a game she walked away, and if he ran after her she growled. Suddenly he was all alone, with nothing much to do until the farmer came back from the fields.

One day he went to the tunnel under the house where the farmer's cat lived and poked his nose in. Up to now he had not paid much attention to the cat. Nor had she paid any attention to him, except to growl sometimes when she walked past him on her way to the barn. They were not really friends. Yet they were not really enemies either, and even her company would be better than none at all.

There was not a sound inside the tunnel. Perhaps the cat was not there. The hole was too small for him to squeeze through, but it could be made bigger. With his paws he scratched away some of the earth and tried once more to get in, only to be greeted by a spitting hiss that made him fall over backward. Then the cat came out, glaring at him, and in the middle of the yard she sat down to wash her face.

She certainly was not friendly, but maybe he could have a game with her anyway. Circling around her, he barked and beat his paws on the ground, inviting her to play. She just stalked past him, went into the barn, and leaped up on a rack of hay.

He was not very good at jumping. Try as he would he could not join her there. At last he gave up and went back to the tunnel, thinking he might dig some more. Then he changed his mind and decided to go exploring around the other side of the house where he had never been before. That was how he found the rabbits.

He could not really play with them because they were in a cage, but if he barked on one side of the cage they all hopped to the other, and by running back and forth he could chase them around and around. It had been more fun playing with his brother and sister, but this was better than being growled at by the cat, or just sitting doing nothing. So every morning after that he went around the house to make the rabbits hop for a while.

Almost always the farmer stayed in the fields until noon, but one day he came home early and found Hi Fella playing with the rabbits. At first he seemed to be laughing, and Hi Fella worked even harder at chasing the rabbits, for he liked to please the farmer. But it turned out the farmer was not laughing. He was sputtering with rage.

4

"You! Bad dog! Get away from those rabbits! You want to scare them to death?"

The big hands reached down and grabbed Hi Fella and carried him to the barn.

For a while he stayed quiet, trying to figure out why he had been shut in the barn, and why he had been called Bad Dog. Then he started crying and scratching at the door, while on the other side his mother barked and whined. Between them they made so much noise that the farmer's wife came to see what was wrong, and she let him out.

That made everything all right. His mother washed his face and fussed over him and even lay down so that he could be with her for a while. With his nose buried in her fur he forgot about the rabbits and the farmer being angry, and he was happy again.

But the next day was worse than ever. On her morning walk in the field his mother had stepped on a bee. When she came back to the barn, Hi Fella thought the way she was limping was a new kind of game and he leaped upon her, only to get snapped at and growled at. Hobbling off, she snarled a warning for him not to follow.

He stared at her, wondering whether he should run after her and nip at her heels, just to be mean. Then he remembered the rabbits and went to play with them instead.

There were some very small ones in the cage. If he could manage to get one out it might be fun to carry it around for a while. By scratching and biting at the wire, he managed to make a hole big enough for his paw to go through. Then he ran around to the other side and barked, and as soon as the rabbits were huddled near the hole he hurried back to shove his paw in. And suddenly he was seized by the farmer's big hand.

This time his mother did not help him get out of the barn. She was in the orchard, lying under a tree, trying to lick the bee stinger out of her paw. All by himself he whined and barked and howled, while in the house the farmer talked with his wife.

"We'll have to get rid of him."

"But he's only a puppy. He just doesn't know better."

"Yes, but we can't take a chance on losing those rabbits. Besides, his mother doesn't want him around anymore. She's about ready to breed again."

"Maybe Ed Travers would take him. He just lost his old cow dog."

"That's a good idea. I'll call him right away."

2

When the barn door opened Hi Fella was afraid he would be called Bad Dog again, but the farmer was no longer angry.

"Come on, you're going to a nice new home, and maybe you will learn to chase cows instead of rabbits."

Near the farmer's feet was a large box. Hi Fella liked boxes, so he sniffed at this one and stood on his hind legs to peer in. It was quite empty, except for a piece of quilt spread over the bottom. He looked at the farmer to make sure he was doing nothing wrong

8

and hopped in, and while he was busy snuffling around, the farmer's wife joined them.

"Here, give him this bone. Then maybe he won't mind the long trip so much."

He had never seen such a big bone. Crouching in a corner of the box he started gnawing on it, until suddenly everything grew dark. The top of the box had closed.

For a moment he was frightened. Then the closed box seemed like a fine place to enjoy the bone without having someone — his mother, for instance — take it away. Again he started gnawing, and again he had to stop. Now the box was tipping, this way and that, as the farmer tied cord around it. Then it rose and floated through the air.

It was not a good place after all, and he had to get out. There were several small holes cut in one side. He tried to shove a paw through one of the holes, lost his balance, and slid into a corner, with the bone underneath him and the quilt on top of him. The box was a terrible place.

He yelped. The box grated over something solid, then stopped moving, and he heard the farmer and his wife talking outside.

"Are you sure he'll be safe in the back of the truck like that, without any tailgate? Couldn't you take him up in front with you?"

"No room. The cab is full of tools."

Hi Fella barked to let them know where he was, thinking they surely would let him out. Something banged, and all at once there was a fearful roar, coming from underneath and all around him. The box started bouncing up and down. The bone kept rolling around and hitting him. He whined and howled, but the truck was making so much noise that he could hardly hear himself.

The road the farmer was driving on went over several hills. As the truck climbed the first steep slope the box slid back. Then it slid forward going down the other side.

On the second hill the road did not go to the very top but cut across the side of it, with a cliff to the left, a deep gully to the right. About halfway up there was a sharp curve, and just there a rock had fallen down from the cliff. Driving around the bend the farmer saw the rock, but not in time to avoid it.

The left front tire went over the rock. The truck bounced up in the air. The box in back leaped off the floor, skidded to the very edge, balanced there for a moment, and tumbled off.

Down into the gully it went, turning end over end, until it came to rest near the bottom, leaning against a tree.

3

Ed Travers was waiting near his barn when the farmer drove in.

"Bring the dog back here. I've fixed a pen for him in the barn."

The farmer went around the side of the truck, and stared in disbelief.

"He's gone! He was in a box back here, and it's gone! It must have fallen off. If it's in the middle of the road and another car comes along — "

"But there's not much traffic. If you hurry you might find him."

The farmer drove back over the way he had come, checking both sides of the road. Every so often he stopped the truck and got out and called.

"Here dog! Hi fella!"

There was no answer, and no sign of the box.

Finally he came to the curve where he had driven over the rock, and he remembered how the truck had bounced, so he spent some time here searching through the brush. Again he called. But now a wind had come up, making the leaves on the trees rustle so that it was hard to hear anything else. He gave up and went on, and at last arrived at a place where he remembered he had looked back and had seen the box still on the truck.

How could a box of that size just disappear? He thought of returning to the curve to search some more, but by this time it had grown so dark that he had to turn on his lights. What chance was there of finding a dog, especially a black dog, on a dark night if he had no idea of where to look?

When he got home he told his wife what he thought must have happened.

"I'll bet someone picked him up. I'll bet a car came along and they saw the box and found him."

"Oh, I hope so!"

"It must be. Otherwise I'd have found him myself. He's a cute fella. Probably they fell in love with him right away and decided to keep him."

"Well, wherever he is, I hope he has a real good home."

4

While the box was tumbling down the hill, Hi Fella protected himself as well as he could by rolling into a ball, but the big bone kept hitting him. By the time the box came to rest he was so battered that he lay quite limp, as if all life had gone out of him.

Finally he opened one eye. Then he moved his legs a little, and opened the other eye. The box was tilted so that he was squashed into a corner, with the bone on top of him and the quilt wound around his legs. He squirmed to get free, and managed to scramble to his feet.

One side of the box had split open a little. He put his nose to the crack and sniffed. No good farm smells came to him, only the scent of dry leaves and damp earth.

To let everyone know where he was, he barked. If his mother did not hear, at least the farmer or the farmer's wife should. He waited, but no footsteps approached. He seemed to be all alone.

Clawing at the crack, he made it big enough for a paw to go through. Outside, the paw waved in the air. Nothing bit it or grabbed it, so he worked some more on the hole he had made, until he could squeeze through. Then he stood staring at his surroundings.

All about him stood great old trees, so tall that their branches arched high over his head. The ground was covered with a thick carpet of pine needles and dry leaves. To his right there were some big clumps of ferns; to his left, bushes and spindly young trees. Beyond them was the hill down which he had fallen.

In one of the trees a bird squawked at him and flapped its wings. He watched it fly away, then limped over to a clump of ferns and lay down. The fronds were not much of a shelter, but he felt a little safer under them.

He dozed, then lifted his head to listen. Far away somewhere, somebody seemed to be calling his name. He thought of the farmer and started to answer, but just then a gust of wind swept through the trees, making the leaves rustle so that he could hear nothing else.

Going back to the box he walked in widening circles, trying to pick up a scent. The farmer's did not seem to be anywhere, but there were many others. Most were unfamiliar to him, but one he knew quite well. Not too long ago a field mouse had passed this way.

Once, back at the farm, he had caught a field mouse in the tall grass next to the barn. He had pounced on it, taken it in his mouth, and very carefully put it down at the farmer's feet. Instinct had told him this was the proper thing to do. The farmer had patted his head and called him Good Dog.

"You'd make a fine retriever, just like your mother. Too bad I don't have any time to go hunting."

Now he followed the trail of the mouse, thinking that if he caught it the farmer would be there to take it and call him Good Dog, just as before. But the scent went only to a small tunnel under a big rock. He

shoved his nose into the tunnel, sneezed and backed away, and started snuffling along some of the other scents.

All of them seemed to go in the same direction, toward a thicket so dense it was almost like a wall. He went that way too, found a well-beaten path that took him right through the wall, and came out on the edge of a stream.

Wading around in the water, he drank until he spied a fish. It was gulping at something on the surface, moving so lazily that he was sure he could catch it. He pounced, making a great splash, and got only a mouthful of water. The fish had vanished. In disgust he hauled himself back on dry land.

The fish had reminded him that he was hungry. By this time the farmer's wife would have put food down on the back steps, and maybe bones too. That reminded him of the bone he had left in the box, and he went back to crawl in.

The bone was still there, but he did not trust the box. Any moment it might start moving again. By pushing and pulling, he managed to get the big bone through the hole. Then he dragged it over to the clump of ferns where he had rested earlier and gnawed on it until most of the meat was gone.

The woods had grown quite black. Night had come, and suddenly he was afraid. The farmer had always shut him in the barn at night. He should be there now, with his mother.

His mouth opened, and out came a long howl. It scared him so that his fur bristled. What had crept closer while he was making that noise?

He listened, and thought he heard a rustling in the bushes. Then there was a sharp squeak, followed by a crunching sound. Whatever was over there must have caught something, maybe the mouse he had tracked earlier.

When it had finished with the mouse, would it come after him? Stealthily he padded away, only to turn and come back again. Something told him that the barn was far off, and his only refuge on this night was the box that smelled of home. Near it he squatted with the bone between his paws, staring into the darkness, ready to defend himself and his one possession.

But whatever had been in the bushes must have gone away. Now everything was quiet. His eyes closed. His head sank down to rest on the bone, and he slept.

5

In his dreams he tumbled over and over inside the box. Then he was back at the farm, and his mother was trying to take the bone away from him. He growled, and opened his eyes to find it was not his mother tugging at the bone. He was face to face, almost nose to nose, with a stranger.

The stranger was smaller than he was, and also black, except for a white stripe down each side of its body and a white tip on its bushy tail. Its scent was unfamiliar, yet not entirely so. Once his mother had come home smelling powerfully like that, and the farmer had been very angry. For days his mother had not been allowed anywhere near the house.

The stranger's beady black eyes stared into his. It knew he was awake, yet it did not seem to be at all afraid. Again it yanked at the bone.

Practically all the meat was gone. The bone was hardly worth fighting over, but it belonged to him, and he would not give it up. He growled again, but the stranger made no move to go away. Instead it went into a peculiar dance, shuffling back and forth, drumming its little forefeet on the ground.

Such a foolish creature needed to be taught a lesson. Baring his teeth, Hi Fella lunged and snapped, and at once found out why the stranger was not afraid. Instantly its rear jerked around, and from under its tail spurted a liquid that shot straight into his eyes. The stuff burned like fire and covered him with such a stench that he could hardly breathe.

Now all he wanted to do was get away, but he could not see. With tears streaming from his eyes he rammed into trees, stumbled over roots, bumped into rocks, floundered through brush, finally reached the stream, and plunged in.

Down and down he went, until the water closed over his head. That brought him back to his senses and washed the worst of the pain out of his eyes.

He coughed and gagged and was sick. Then he dragged himself out of the stream and lay on the bank.

There he spent the rest of the night, wet and shivering, sick and miserable, thinking with longing of his good safe bed of hay in the barn.

6

The warmth of the sun woke him. For a moment he could not figure out where he was. Then the way he smelled reminded him of his encounter with the awful stranger the night before. But by this time he was so used to the smell that it did not bother him anymore. He no longer felt sick. In fact, he was hungry.

Thinking of the scraps the farmer's wife would give him, he walked along the bank of the stream, heading south. Instinct told him that home was to the south, so that was the way he had to go: downstream.

After a while he came to a place where the water

spread into a wide pond. Here the shore was so spongy that his paws sank deep, making a sucking sound each time he pulled them out. Turning to escape from this muck, he jumped back in alarm as something whisked past his nose and plopped into the water. A moment later its head rose not far away, and he saw it was a frog, like those back at the farm, only much bigger.

He sniffed at the place where it had been and did not like the scent very much. Still, a frog was something to eat, and he was very hungry. So he waded into the water and pounced, and only made a big splash. The frog had got away.

Then he saw there were a lot more frogs, squatting all along the bank. He ran and pounced, ran and pounced, and had no luck at all. The sucking of his paws in and out of the mud gave the frogs warning.

Finally he sat very still, and some of the frogs came back to rest their heads on the bank. One crawled all the way out of the water to squat right in front of him. Once more he pounced, and there was the frog, cold and slippery and squirming, under his paws.

Carefully he took it into his mouth. One leg slid down his throat, where it tickled. Shifting the frog around, he tried to get the leg out, but instead another went down, and both of them started kicking.

That made him cough so the frog fell out. On the ground it lay as if dead, until he sniffed at it. Then in a great curving leap it sailed up and away, to plop back in the pond.

Anyway, it had not really appealed to him.

Now the sun was directly overhead and very hot. In the shade of a tree he lay down, twitched his ears to get rid of some flies, and put his head on his paws.

Soon he began sucking. He was a little puppy again, drinking his mother's milk. Then he heard the farmer's wife calling. He raced with his mother to the bowl of food, and once there he raced some more, trying to beat her to the bottom where the meat was.

The dinner bell rang, calling the farmer from the fields. He and his mother ran to meet him, leaping over the tall grass — and he woke up.

Instead of bounding through the field he was lying near the pond. The air was heavy, and very still. There was not a sound anywhere, except the ringing cry of one bird. That was the bell he had heard in his dream.

From the sky to his left came a rumble that sent a tingle of fear down his spine. Whenever they heard this sound, he and his mother had always taken shelter in the barn, where they would be safe from the storm.

Now where could he find shelter? Without any

place to go he started running along the edge of the pond, not caring how he splashed through the mud. The closer the thunder came the faster he ran, until he was plastered with mud from head to tail.

A gust of wind sent ripples over the pond. A few drops of rain fell. Then the rumbles drifted away, and soon the sun was shining again. The storm had turned and gone toward the north.

Now there was no longer any reason to keep running, but somehow he could not stop. On and on he went, slopping through the mud, wanting only to get home.

7

When he saw the house he stopped and stared. There was a woman sitting on the porch. He thought of running straight to her, but something told him to be careful. The house did not look like the farmer's house, and the woman did not look like the farmer's wife.

Staying hidden in the bushes with only his head showing, he tried to speak to the woman. The hoarse croak that came out startled even him, and it had a terrible effect on the woman. She took one look at him and screamed.

"A bear! Right there in the bushes! A bear!"

Hi Fella backed up to hide himself completely. The woman's scream had frightened him, yet he did not want to leave. He was very hungry, and very lonely.

Back at the house a door slammed, and a man spoke.

"Where? I don't see anything."

"Over there. I only saw the head. All dirty, full of mud. Terrible looking."

"Smells a lot like skunk to me."

Hi Fella heard footsteps coming toward the bushes and wagged his tail, expecting the man to call him. He would run out and the people would fuss over him and pat his head and put down scraps for him to eat, and everything would be all right again.

Near the bushes the footsteps stopped, and the next minute a rock came crashing through the leaves, landing so close to him that he yelped.

"Why, it's only a dog! I'm sorry, dog! Here dog, here dog!"

The man kept calling, but Hi Fella did not hear. He was bounding off through the woods, as fast as he could go. Only when he was far away from the house did he stop to hide in a thicket. He could not understand why the people had chased him, nor could he understand why they were strangers, instead of the farmer and his wife.

His paws were beginning to bleed. Hunger made him dizzy. Yet as soon as he had caught his breath and stopped trembling he set out again, going south, walking in a wide circle around the house where for some reason he had not been welcome.

Late in the afternoon he came to another house. He prowled cautiously around this one, drawn to it but afraid to go close. Finally he sat under some bushes just at the edge of the woods, where he had a good view of the back door.

The sun was low in the sky. Long shadows lay across the yard, and everything glowed in a strange reddish light. Soon it would be night again.

He raised his head and sniffed. A wonderful smell of food was coming from the house. He did not dare to go to the door and beg, but maybe if he just waited the farmer's wife would come out with some scraps.

The red glow faded. A blue haze spread over the ground. Lights went on inside the house.

He caught a glimpse of the woman passing by a window, and his tail thumped on the ground. Any minute now she would call him. He heard the clatter of dishes and two voices, a man's and a woman's. They did not sound at all like those of the farmer and his wife.

A light snapped on over the back door, and the woman came out with a big dish. Hi Fella jumped up, whipping his tail from side to side. Even though she was not the farmer's wife he almost ran to her.

But she did not put the dish down near the steps. Instead she opened a large can, dumped into it what was in the dish, put the cover back on the can, and went back inside. A moment later the light over the back door snapped off.

Well, he would wait for a while, then go to the can and take what she had left there. He wriggled into a more comfortable position and stared at the house.

Another light appeared, coming through a front window of the house. The light in back went out. That made the yard nice and dark, so he would not be seen. But halfway to the house he was stopped in his tracks by a fearful racket: voices yelling, thumpings, and loud explosions, all coming from inside the house.

Somehow it did not sound quite real, but more as if the people had turned it on, and once he got used to it he felt even safer. As long as they listened to that noise, they were not likely to hear any he might make. Boldly he went to the can and sniffed. He could smell the food, but there seemed to be no way to get to it. Around and around the can he went, snuffling and pawing.

8

With his mind on the food, he never even noticed someone coming up behind him until he heard a snort. Whirling around, he faced a round, wooly, gray-brown animal with strange black patches over its eyes, that rocked from side to side and growled at him ferociously. He knew why. It owned the can.

Slowly he backed away, and at once the other one calmed down. Standing on its hind legs, it gave the can a big push. The can fell, and as it rolled clanking over the ground the other one made for the woods, bouncing almost like a rubber ball. Hi Fella ran too, but in a different direction.

For a while after that nothing more happened. The noise inside the house went on. Everything outside stayed quiet. Then Hi Fella saw a shadow slip across the yard toward the can.

This other one had paws that were almost like hands. In no time it had the cover off the can and was raking out what was inside. Hi Fella crept closer, spied a piece of meat, grabbed it, and ran.

At a safe distance he gulped down the meat. Then he went back, to find the other one sitting on its haunches nibbling a slice of bread held between its front paws. This time it just glanced at him mildly, so he nosed around picking out what he liked: a few more meat scraps, a boiled potato, and a bone.

Finally everything that had been in the can was gone, except for some empty cartons and waste paper. The other one tore these into little pieces and carefully poked them under the can. Then it shuffled away.

Picking up his bone, Hi Fella tagged along. The other one went to the stream in front of the house and drank. He put down the bone and drank too, until the other one started to leave. Then he snatched up the bone and followed again.

The other one went this way, that way, all through

the woods. Every once in a while it stopped to dig a hole and pull out something that it ate. When it had gone on, Hi Fella put down the bone to sniff at each hole, but there was never anything in them, and he had to hurry to catch up. He was determined not to lose this new companion.

The sky in the east lightened, and birds started twittering. This seemed to be a signal for the other one. It went to a tall tree and climbed the trunk, and near the top it suddenly disappeared.

Hi Fella tried his claws on the trunk, but he could not climb. For a while he stood waiting, thinking the other one would come down again. At last he yawned, turned around a few times, and settled down at the foot of the tree, with the bone between his paws.

His head nodded, then jerked up. From under a nearby rock one of those pesky chipmunks had popped out to scold him. Back at the farm he at least would have chased it up a tree. Now he only stared at it sleepily, put his head down on the bone, and slept.

9

The sun was just overhead when he woke. He looked around, but the other one was nowhere in sight. He sniffed along its trail, which took him first to the stream, then to the house where they had met the night before. The other one was not there, either, but two people were. A woman was standing on the steps, and a man was just putting a big rock on top of the garbage can.

"There. No raccoon could get in the can with this heavy rock on it."

"Let's hope not. I'm getting awfully tired of cleaning up such a mess every morning."

They went into the house, and a little later they were in front of it, splashing in the stream.

Hi Fella went to the can and pushed, but it had become very heavy. No matter how hard he shoved, it would not budge.

At last he gave up trying and went back to the raccoon's tree. Now that the sun was shining on it he could see a hollow near the top, just where the raccoon had vanished the night before. He scratched on the bark and whined, but there was no answer from the hollow, so he wandered over to dig under the big rock, to see if he could make the chipmunk come out. Nothing happened there, either. All through the woods everything was quiet, and the day was very warm. It made him feel lazy.

He flopped down and was just dozing off when the chipmunk whisked past his nose to dive under the rock. Without bothering to get up, he barked a couple of times. The chipmunk stuck its head out to bark back in a shrill little voice, but he pretended not to hear. Chipmunks always teased that way just when he did not feel like moving.

At last the air cooled. The sun disappeared. The blue haze spread through the woods. In the treetops the evening birds began to sing. One in the raccoon's tree squawked and flew away. Then pieces of bark started falling, and there was the raccoon, coming headfirst down the trunk.

Hi Fella jumped up, wagging his tail. Without even looking at him the raccoon went shuffling off toward the stream. Once there it lay on a flat rock to dip its paws in the water. Then slowly it slid in and began wading upstream, patting its paws all along the bottom as if hunting for something.

Hi Fella slipped in too, and walked around to let the water wash through his fur. When he crawled out he felt quite a bit cleaner, and cooler, and very hungry. But the raccoon stayed in the stream until all light was gone from the sky. Then it came on shore and led the way to the people's house.

There everything was the same as the night before. The people had turned on their noise. The light was on in front. The yard was dark. But when the raccoon pushed, the garbage can did not fall over.

Standing on its hind legs, the raccoon walked all around the can, feeling the rock on top. Then it dropped down to feel around the bottom, until it came to a place where the ground was uneven, leaving a small space under the can. There it began to dig.

As earth was flung away the can began to tip a bit, and a bit more, and more. With a scraping noise the

rock started sliding. Just in time the raccoon jumped aside, and as the two of them bounded away there was a great crash.

Under the bushes they waited, side by side for the first time. It seemed the people surely must have heard that awful racket. But just then their own noise happened to be even louder than usual. Finally the raccoon went back to the can and pulled off the cover.

On this night there were many good things to eat: fish and crackers, bread and potatoes, some creamed spinach, and a piece of cake that the raccoon favored, which gave Hi Fella a chance to eat most of the fish.

Again, after they had finished, the raccoon tidied up. This time it patted all the torn paper into the earth it had dug from under the can. Then they wandered through the woods until dawn, and went back to the den tree.

Now Hi Fella knew what to expect. While the raccoon climbed up to the hollow, he scratched together some leaves to make himself a bed down below.

10

Back at the farm he had slept at night and stayed awake most of the day. The raccoon's hours were hard to get used to. The next noon he was wide awake, with nothing to do but wait for night. So he decided to go to the house and see what the people were doing.

They were outside, sitting on the back steps. The man was putting some wire on the garbage can, while the woman watched.

"There. Now the cover won't come off unless you

snap this catch. When you want to open it all you have to do is—ouch! Just be careful you don't pinch your fingers."

"But won't the raccoon snap the catch?"

"My gosh, a raccoon's not *that* smart!"

The man put the can down beside the steps, and they both went into the house.

Hi Fella stared at the can, wishing the raccoon would come to open it. He was hungry. Finally he went to the stream for a drink to fill his stomach, and lay on a cool rock to wait for dark.

He almost overslept. When he got back to the den tree the raccoon was already climbing down. It looked sleepy and cross, but after his nap Hi Fella wanted to play. Crouching and springing, he bounded around to nip at the raccoon's heels. At first it paid no attention. Then all at once it snorted, and turned on him with such a growl that he almost fell over backward. Yet it did not seem to be really angry, but just telling him to behave, as his mother used to tell him. And just as he had with his mother, he lowered his head and stood still until the raccoon walked on.

At the stream the raccoon paddled for a while, and suddenly dove under a rock to come up with a flapping fish. While Hi Fella watched, waving his tail and licking his chops, the raccoon sat on the bank and ate the fish, until only the tail was left. This it placed on the ground to pat absentmindedly, while it stared at a nearby tree. All at once it bounded away, and Hi Fella downed the fish tail in one gulp.

The raccoon was chasing a tiny mouse up the trunk of the tree. When the mouse reached a branch near the top it ran to the very tip, and the raccoon followed, balancing precariously. One paw reached out. The mouse was almost caught. Then suddenly it was gone. Floating through the air almost as if it had wings, it dropped to a lower branch.

On the higher one the raccoon tried to turn around. Its fat body wobbled more and more. Finally it fell off, but it managed to hook one paw and pull itself back up again. Then it crawled down and out on the lower branch. It seemed determined to catch the mouse.

Again the mouse waited until the very last moment. This time it floated all the way to the ground and scampered off. Snorting with fury, the raccoon came slowly down the trunk, and shuffled toward the people's house.

Everything there was the same as the night before, except that the can fell over right away. But then, no matter how the raccoon tugged, the cover would not come off.

Looking around as if not the least bit interested in

what it was doing, the raccoon ran its paws all over the cover. It found the wire and fingered that, pushing and pulling, until there was a loud snap.

Both Hi Fella and the raccoon ran for the bushes, but nothing else happened. The can stayed quiet. The people did not come out of the house. So they went back, and now the raccoon had no trouble pulling off the cover.

This night the people had given them almost half a cherry pie, several slices of bread, some spaghetti in a can, chunks of fat and meat, two potatoes, and two bones.

While the raccoon ate the pie, Hi Fella concentrated on the meat and fat, until out of the corner of his eyes he saw a small figure coming toward them.

It was the terrible little black and white animal that had sprayed the burning liquid on him.

With a yelp of fear he fled, but the raccoon went on calmly eating. The skunk nosed around, found a piece of fat, and chewed on it. Side by side the two of them ate, so close together that the skunk's plumy tail lay over the raccoon's back.

From a distance Hi Fella watched the skunk down his share of the food. Finally he could stand it no longer and crept closer. The skunk only jerked its tail a little. Keeping a wary eye on his enemy, he grabbed a potato and, after that, a bone.

By this time the cherry pie was gone and the raccoon was busy with the can of spaghetti. Squatting on its haunches, it lifted out the strands one by one to nibble daintily.

At last there was no more spaghetti, and it stuck its head into the can to lick the sauce. Then it began acting peculiar. The can on its head started going around and around and up and down, while the raccoon's body went through all kinds of crazy motions, humping and bucking, turning in circles, even hopping backward.

The skunk dodged and scuttled off. Hi Fella leaped to get out of the way. The raccoon seemed to have gone completely mad. It even clanked the can against the side of the house. But finally it quieted down. Sitting on its rump, it took the can between its forepaws and yanked. And all of a sudden the can popped off, to hit the house with a bang.

Now the raccoon was a sorry sight, with spaghetti sauce all over its coat. Without even bothering to tidy up it marched straight off through the woods. Hi Fella started to follow, remembered the bone, and went back for it. When he caught up again, the raccoon was already climbing the trunk of the den tree. On this night they did no wandering.

11

For a few days after that, everything was peaceful. In the afternoon Hi Fella always went to the house to see what the people were doing. Sometimes they were splashing in the stream. Sometimes he could hear them talking and moving around inside. Once the woman was in the yard, hanging things on a line. Nothing more was done to the garbage can.

Then one day the man was sitting on the back steps, rubbing his hand over a long stick, and the woman was sitting nearby, watching.

"But it's cruel. And it's against the law. You're not allowed to shoot raccoons this time of year."

"Who'll know? I'll just throw it back in the woods somewhere and nobody will be the wiser. Well, I'd better try out the sight. See the knot in that tree over there? If the gun's sighted right, I should be able to hit it."

The woman put her hands over her ears. The man raised the stick to his shoulder, and there was a terrible explosion. Hi Fella jumped straight into the air, then ran like mad, while the man yelled.

"How's that for a good shot? Right in the middle of the knot!"

The noise had been so terrifying that for the rest of the day Hi Fella hid in a thicket far from the house. Even when the sky darkened he was afraid to move, until hunger drove him back to the den tree.

The raccoon had already left the tree, and left the stream, and was on the way to the people's house. On this night it seemed to be in an especially bad mood. When Hi Fella approached from behind, it whipped around and lunged at him with a ferocious snarl.

A bright moon shone through the trees, making patches of the woods almost as light as day. That seemed to be the reason for the raccoon's ill humor. Whenever it came to one of the moonlit patches it growled and shuffled through in a hurry, as if it feared the light.

When they got to the house Hi Fella's own fear returned. Something was wrong. The light had not been turned on in front, nor had the people switched on their noise. The whole place was silent and dark, except for the back yard, which was bathed in moonlight.

At the edge of the woods the raccoon sat down and growled. Hi Fella also felt they were not alone. Somewhere nearby something was waiting for them to come out of the shadows.

Finally the raccoon took a few steps toward the house, but stopped just at the edge of the moonlight and came back again. Hi Fella could smell the food in the can. He gulped, and the raccoon snorted. Then for a long time both of them sat very still.

A small glow appeared in the doorway of the house. It shone for only a moment, and Hi Fella knew what it was. He had seen such a glow before, when the farmer had lit a cigarette. It was nothing to be afraid of, but it did betray the presence of someone in the doorway.

At once the raccoon slipped away. Hi Fella stayed behind until he caught a whiff of smoke. Then he hurried off to join the raccoon.

Three times during the night they made the trip back to the house and stole away again. Once they saw a small figure drift across the yard, the white stripes on its pelt gleaming in the moonlight. It went to the can, sniffed around, and drifted away again.

On their fourth visit there was a change. The moonlight was gone. The yard was dark. And whatever had been waiting in the doorway was gone too.

Without hesitation the raccoon went to the can, knocked it over, pulled off the cover, and raked out what was inside: baked potatoes, scraps of roast beef, carrots, and chocolate pudding.

By the time they had finished eating, the sky in the east was light. So they went directly to the den tree and directly to sleep.

12

When Hi Fella arrived the next day, the people were picking up scraps of paper. The man looked cross.

"Practically all night I sat there waiting, and all I see is a skunk."

"Maybe it's a skunk that makes this mess."

"Nah, a skunk wouldn't be strong enough to knock over a garbage can. Listen, here comes a car. Maybe that's the game warden now."

The man who got out of the car was carrying a box.

"You the people having trouble with the raccoon?"

"Yeah, just look. Every night the garbage can is knocked over and everything's scattered around."

"Well, I think we can take care of that. This here's a box trap. I'll show you how it works. You pull up this door and fasten it to the catch up here. Put some bait inside, way back, so the coon will have to go all the way in to get it. Put a little on the pan, and a little just in front of the trap, to sort of coax the coon in. As soon as it steps on the pan, the catch is released and the door comes down and locks. For bait, use just what you'd put in the garbage can, and put the box right where the can usually is."

"If it's caught, what happens to it? Does it have to be killed?"

"Of course not. I can take it to the game farm and they'll either keep it there or release it somewhere else. Just give me a ring when it's caught, and I'll come pick it up."

After the car had driven away and the people had gone into the house, Hi Fella stared and stared at the box. He did not like it. It reminded him of another box that had tumbled down a hill with him inside. Yet no matter how closely he watched, this one did not move at all.

That night when he and the raccoon paid their usual visit, the box was still sitting there and the garbage can was gone. The house was quiet. There was a light in front, but the people had not turned on their noise.

The raccoon eyed the box for such a long time that Hi Fella grew restless. He whined, and the raccoon growled. Then they were silent.

Finally the light over the door of the house snapped on. The man came out, looked at the box, then went back inside, and the light snapped off. A moment later the noise started inside the house. That seemed to reassure the raccoon. Slipping across the yard, it picked up a piece of cake lying in front of the box.

Hi Fella prowled around, smelling meat. But whenever he tried to enter the box the raccoon growled and drove him away. He was supposed to wait until it got the stuff out of the box.

The raccoon ate slowly, turning the cake around and around, and once the cake was gone it had to pick up every crumb on the ground. Finally it looked inside the box, but growled and backed away. It was afraid to go in.

Hi Fella edged closer, thinking now he might get the meat. But again the raccoon chased him away. Snorting with fear, it poked its head through the opening. Nothing happened. Very slowly it crept forward until it was entirely inside the box. Then

something snapped, something hit Hi Fella on the nose, and the opening was gone. The box was closed.

Inside, the raccoon started making a terrible racket, growling and snarling and screaming, while it flung its body around so that the box actually shook. Hi Fella ran off, but returned when the commotion stopped.

Now the raccoon was carefully searching for a way to get out. Its paws rustled all along the sides of the box, the top, the bottom. Under the door there was a fairly wide crack. Long brown fingers poked through the crack to slip from one end to the other. Hi Fella went close and sniffed at the crack, and suddenly the light over the door of the house snapped on. He barely had time to reach the bushes before the man came out.

"Hey, we got it! The trap is shut. Hurry up, call the game warden. Tell him we got it!"

The man went back into the house, but the light stayed on.

From his hiding place Hi Fella heard a soft scratching, and saw a brown paw pushing through the crack, first in one place, then in another. He whined, and from inside the box came an answer, a sad little *chirrrr* that sounded like both a call for help and an offer of friendship. It drew him out of hiding, straight across the brightly lit yard.

Standing over the box he whimpered, and again the raccoon trilled an answer. He sniffed at a corner, then started chewing on it.

The wood was hard. He managed to pry loose a splinter, tore it off, and continued gnawing. In the box the raccoon was very quiet, as if it understood what he was doing. Finally he had made a small hole, just at the end of the crack. When he shoved his nose in he could smell the meat, the leafy scent of the raccoon's fur, and the odor of the people, all mixed together.

He had forgotten all about the light over the door, but all at once another, brighter light roared toward him, coming from two glaring eyes on the road. Again he had to run and hide.

The eyes were the headlights of a car that stopped near the house. A man got out and went to the box and was bending over it when the people came out.

"Well, now, look here. Look how this corner has been chewed. You know, I thought I saw an animal running off as I drove up."

"You mean there's nothing in the trap?"

"Oh, there's something in it, all right. Fairly heavy."

"But there's not a sound."

"Yeah, they're usually quiet when you come to check the trap. Sort of pretending they're not there, you know. What I can't figure out is how that corner got chewed. From outside, and not by any raccoon. Those tooth marks look more like—I'd almost say a dog's."

"A dog and a raccoon? They'd never run together."

"Not too likely. But I remember reading a while back about how a lost dog and a raccoon spent a whole winter together. So it could happen. Anyway, we got this rascal, all right. I'll take it to the farm first thing in the morning."

The people watched the game warden put the trap in the car, then watched as the headlights bounced away. After the roar of the engine had died away in the distance, the woman put her hand on the man's arm.

"Listen. I just heard something back there in the bushes. It sounded like a dog crying."

"Nonsense. The game warden mentions a dog, and right away you think you hear a dog. Come on, there's nothing back there."

They went into the house. The door closed. The light snapped off. The yard was dark again, and very still.

After a while the people turned on their noise, and Hi Fella knew it was safe for him to come out of hiding. Yet for a long time he did not move. Always the raccoon had decided what they should do. Left alone, he had a hard time making up his mind to anything at all.

He had seen the man carry off the box, but he could not believe the raccoon was gone. All he had to do was hunt, and he would surely find it somewhere. Going to the spot where the box had been, he snuffled around and picked up the raccoon's scent, but it only led him back to the bushes. The game warden's trail smelled faintly of the raccoon, so he followed that, but it went only a short distance and ended in an unpleasant smell of gasoline.

Perhaps the raccoon had gone to the stream. He would find it there paddling in the water. It might even catch a fish and leave the tail for him. He was very hungry.

Near the stone on which the raccoon always lay before slipping into the stream, he stood looking up and down and listening. Nothing moved anywhere. Except for the soft rippling of the water, there was not a sound.

At last the sky grew light and the birds began to sing.

Now the raccoon would be up in the den tree. He left the stream and went to the tree and curled up at its base. All he had to do was wait. As soon as night came again he would hear the claws up above, and bits of bark would fall, and the raccoon would climb down looking sleepy and cross. And when they went to the people's house they would find the garbage can full of a lot of especially good things.

In his dreams he ate and ate, and he was still hungry.

13

The following afternoon he was jerked out of sleep by a loud noise.

Wind was blowing so hard that it made his fur stand on end. Leaves scuttled wildly over the ground, slapped against him, and swirled away. The sky was almost as black as night, except when a bright light streaked across. Then there would be another long rumble like the one that had awakened him.

He looked up into the den tree, hoping the raccoon would come down. Without its guidance he had no

58

idea of where to go to find shelter from the storm. But all at once a blinding light exploded right beside him, and he had to run. He ran and ran, yet no matter which way he went the lightning seemed to pursue. It crackled on all sides.

Then there was a sudden lull in the storm. The wind died down. Not a leaf rustled. The lightning still flickered but made no noise. The earth seemed to be holding its breath.

He held his too, listening to something far away that sounded like millions of flies buzzing. The buzzing came swiftly closer, turned into a high whine, and from that into a mighty roar. On his left a tree fell down. A wall of wind slammed against him, picked him up, and hurled him through the air along with leaves and branches and torrents of rain.

He was flung against something solid. Things flew over and past him. Rain swirled down, beating harder and harder, changing to cold white balls that felt like stones hitting him. They covered his body and piled up all around him.

Then, as quickly as it had come, the storm was gone. The roaring wind swept away. The hail stopped. Everything grew quiet. Daylight came back, and soon the sun was shining.

For a long time he lay without moving. The terrible noise still buzzed in his ears. He felt numb and cold, and his whole body ached. At last he opened his eyes, to find he was lying in a hole made by an uprooted tree, with a great wall of tangled roots towering over him. That was what had saved him from the full force of the wind.

He got to his feet and shook himself, sending a shower of the white balls clattering over those that lay on the ground. He took a few steps, and clambered out of the hole. One of his legs hurt. He limped about, trying to get his bearings, and thought the raccoon's den must be somewhere over to the right.

Fallen trees barred the way, and everywhere the ground was littered with branches that he had to crawl over or under. At last he was on familiar ground, but everything looked strange. Where the den tree had been, a great gap let the sky show through. The tree was gone.

It lay on the ground, broken in three pieces. The top had split apart to lay open the raccoon's nest of leaves and shredded bark and fur. The familiar leafy scent was so strong that it seemed the raccoon must be there, but it was not.

He thought of the people's house and limped in that direction, only to find changes there too. The bushes under which he and the raccoon had hidden were flattened by a huge tree fallen across the yard.

The garbage can was gone. The man was at the side of the house, nailing boards over a window. The woman was picking up pieces of broken glass. There was no sign of the raccoon here either.

He went toward the stream, and a terrible roar that sounded like the wind grew louder and louder as he approached. The noise came from the water, rushing by in great waves, so fast that it made him dizzy.

Water boiled over the rock where he had always stood to drink. Waves even lapped against the tree where the raccoon had tried to catch the mouse. A big branch came hurtling downstream, twisting around and around, end over end, and suddenly it bounded toward the shore, looking alive, like a charging animal.

He turned and fled, back to the fallen den tree. There he settled down on the damp earth, with his head resting on what had been the raccoon's bed. The scent was comforting. Yet for a long time he could not stop shivering.

14

The sky was still light when he got up to stand watch. Whenever a breeze rustled through the leaves he thought it might be the raccoon coming home, and his tail began to wave.

But night came, the woods grew quite dark, and the raccoon did not appear.

Pacing around and around the fallen tree, he whined. Then he barked, once, twice, and stopped to listen. Nothing answered. He barked again. And finally he was barking steadily, like a drum beating. Only when his eyes caught a flicker of light showing through the trees did he stop.

Slowly the beam came closer. It disappeared for an instant, shone again, grew brighter, swept this way and that, and he heard footsteps crackling toward him. A voice called out.

"Where are you?"

He knew he had to leave. Any moment a rock might come crashing through the brush, or the man's gun would explode. Stealthily he slipped away, but a fallen branch lay in his path. His sore leg bumped into it, and he yelped.

At once the voice called out again.

"Dog? Are you hurt?"

The light swept dangerously close. He crouched down, hardly breathing, and the man stayed quiet too, probably waiting for him to make another move. But finally he spoke.

"Come on. Let me know where you are. I only want to help you."

Again there was silence. Then came a piercing whistle, so sudden, so terrifying, that Hi Fella jumped and fell against the branch. Immediately the light jerked toward him, shining directly into his eyes, blinding him for a moment. The next instant he was plunging wildly away, through brush, over and under fallen trees, paying no attention to the pain in his leg or to which way he was going.

Not until the menace of the light was far behind did he dare stop to check on his surroundings. The part of the woods he had come to showed little damage from the storm. No trees were down, and only a few broken branches lay on the ground. Here traveling would be easier. He lifted his head to test the air, and turned toward the south.

Memory of the farm had grown dim, but still it pulled him to the south. Somewhere there he had had another home, in a barn.

15

All through the rest of that night he walked steadily, only stopping now and then for a drink. For two days he had eaten nothing, yet he was not at all hungry, only very thirsty.

Something was wrong with him. His legs had grown strangely weak, so that he kept stumbling. One minute he was shivering with cold, the next minute he felt burning hot. He could not see very well. Everything around him wavered and blurred.

Shortly after daylight his legs were so shaky that they would not hold him up anymore. At the foot of a tree that looked something like the raccoon's he lay down, to stare with wide-open eyes at all the bushes and trees circling around him. Every bone and every muscle in his body ached. It even hurt to breathe.

His head jerked up. There was the raccoon, just going around a clump of ferns. He struggled to his feet, ran a few steps, and fell. By the time he got up again the raccoon had vanished, but it could not have gone far. He wandered around, looking up in all the trees, until something wet splashed against his legs. He had walked straight into the stream.

Now a dark haze was spreading all about him, as if day were changing into night. With the last of his strength he managed to get out of the water, and collapsed on the bank. There he lay in a thick, swirling fog.

For some time he drifted in the fog. Then he was somewhere else, in the woods, trying to escape from a man who was throwing rocks at him. His legs pumped up and down, faster and faster, yet he stayed in exactly the same spot. The man raised a gun, and a bright light made the earth jump and roar.

His own terrified yelping woke him. He must have slept all through the day and into the night, for now the sky was quite black. He did not know where he was. All he wanted to do was get back home, but he did not know where home was. In a barn somewhere? Or at the foot of a tree? He seemed to be all mixed up, and when he tried to move everything whirled. He could not even raise his head.

Again he drifted in the fog. Then he really was back home, lying with his mother in the bright sunlight. The warmth felt wonderful. It took the chill out of his body, and the ache from his bones. He was not sick any longer. He was hungry.

Basking in the sun, he enjoyed the comfort until his mother began acting peculiar. Very slowly she started circling around him, sniffing as if she could not figure out just what he was.

She snuffled in his ear, and he woke to find he was not home, but still lying near the stream. Yet part of the dream was true. The sun was shining down on him. He did feel much better. And someone was circling around him, only it was not his mother.

Nor was it the raccoon.

This animal was a stranger. Yet it was not entirely strange. Back at the farm he had known an animal something like this: the cat who had lived under the farmer's house. That cat had been slender, with a small head and dainty feet, and its fur had been dark. This cat was tawny in color and much bigger, with a large head, wide shoulders, and a body heavy with muscle. Just as he opened his eyes it started nosing along his foreleg. Then it glanced up, noticed he was awake, and turned away. Its rump was broad and round, and there was no tail. Hopping almost like a rabbit it went to a clump of bushes, and there it squatted, half hidden in the leaves, to stare at him.

With difficulty he managed to get to his feet. Swaying a little, he stared back at the cat, thinking of home. The cat there had not been friendly, but not exactly unfriendly, either. Maybe this one would act the same way.

He took a few shaky steps toward the bushes. The cat blinked its bright green eyes, and from its throat came a low growl, warning him not to come any closer. Obediently he stood still. Then he raised his head to sniff, and turned back to follow a scent that led him to a fallen tree not far away. Hidden under the trunk of the tree were the remains of an animal the cat must have caught and partly eaten.

He had a hard time crawling under the tree to drag out the meat, but once he started eating he could feel strength returning with each bite. When the last morsel was gone he went first to the stream for a drink, and after that to the bushes where the cat had hidden. It was not there any longer. He nosed around to pick up its scent and, with his head down, followed the trail through the woods.

That took him west for a while, then south, and brought him at last to a pile of large boulders. Down near the ground the biggest of these boulders had split apart, to form the entrance to a cave. Here the trail of the cat ended.

He did not dare go in. Just at the entrance of the cave he sat down, and after a while he could hear small rustlings inside.

The cat was in there, moving around.

Knowing it was there made him feel less lonely. Wriggling closer, he ducked his head and stared steadily into the mouth of the cave, until all light faded from the sky.

Now everything inside was quiet, as if the cat might have gone to sleep. He got up and scraped together some leaves, to make a bed something like the one he had had at the foot of the raccoon's tree. Then he turned around a few times and lay down and closed his eyes.

16

Just after the sky lightened, something woke him. One of his eyes opened, and closed again. The cat was moving about inside the cave. It sneezed, rustled closer, and growled. Then it sniffed all around him as it had the day before.

He stayed curled up and kept his eyes closed until the cat seemed satisfied and padded away. Then he got up to stretch and shake the leaves off his coat, but he did not try to follow the cat, remembering how cross the raccoon always had been upon awakening.

Unlike the raccoon, the cat did not shuffle and dawdle. It traveled swiftly, straight through the woods, so that when he decided to go after it he almost had to run to keep it in sight. It seemed to be following a path that led finally to a large clearing. There it stopped and sat down to stare at two buildings some distance away.

The clearing was empty. Nothing moved anywhere. The cat started off again, going to a wire fence, where it flattened down to slip under the lowest strand. Hi Fella tried to do the same thing, but his body was too big. A sharp barb dug into his fur. All he could do was tear loose and back out again.

As the cat disappeared in the tall grass on the other side, he ran along the fence, searching for a way to get through. There seemed to be none, but finally he came to a place where the wire was drawn up to pass over a large rock. That left a hole next to the rock big enough for him to squeeze through, but on the other side he immediately ran into more trouble. Something very large, he had no time to see what, came lumbering toward him.

In panic he tried to find the hole to get out again and could not. The big thing loomed over him, lowered its head, and gave him a push. Then it ambled away, to join two others who were grazing nearby.

It was only a cow, like the one he had known back

at the farm. If he stayed out of the way of the big feet, a cow was harmless enough. Cautiously he circled around these three and went plowing through the grass, hunting for the cat.

There was no trace of it, until suddenly its head appeared above the grass. It seemed to be standing tall to get a better view of something. When he plodded closer it glanced back and hissed at him. Then very slowly it crept forward, placing each paw carefully, exactly in the track of the one before, so that hardly a blade of grass moved.

Its whiskers trembled. Its body wriggled. And all at once, in a great leap, it pounced on a rabbit.

There was no struggle. The rabbit was killed so swiftly that it did not even cry out. Growling softly, the cat dragged the limp body between its legs, straight across the meadow to the foot of a stone wall. There, still growling, it settled down to eat.

Hi Fella stood by watching, gulping and waving his tail.

At last, when the rabbit was about half gone, the cat seemed to lose interest. Circling around, it raked sod over what was left. Then, in one movement so smooth that it might have been flying, it leaped to the top of the stone wall and was at once very busy washing its face.

Hi Fella went to the remains of the rabbit, glancing

up at each step to make sure the cat would not object. He pulled the meat from under the sod. But he had an idea it still belonged to the cat as long as it stayed in that spot, so he moved some distance away before he ate.

The rabbit made a good meal. His hunger was gone. The sun was pleasantly warm. The meadow was peaceful. He flopped down near the wall and closed his eyes. Then he remembered the cat, and jumped up again to make sure it was still sitting on the wall. It was not.

Snuffling around, he tried to pick up its trail, until a gleam of bright fur on the wall caught his eyes. The cat was still there after all, but stretched so flat it was hardly visible. It seemed to be sleeping. Once more he settled down, put his head on his paws, and sighed.

But he could not sleep. In the quiet, lazy meadow too much was going on. The cows wandered here and there. Birds flew down from a big tree to hop and peck, and flew back up again. Grasshoppers snapped all through the grass. Flies buzzed, and bees hummed. Besides, he was afraid the cat might leave without him. Whenever it stirred slightly he half got up, ready to follow if it decided to move.

The cat stayed on the wall a long time, until the sun

slipped behind the big tree and they were in the shade. Then it rose and arched its body in a big stretch, and jumped to the ground. Without even glancing at him it trotted away, across the meadow, leading him to a large pond.

Grasshoppers whirred in all directions to get out of their way. Near the pond the three cows were lying down now, chewing with their eyes closed, half asleep. A few frogs squawked and splashed into the water, making rings that spread wider and wider.

At the edge of the pond the cat stepped on a stone and lapped delicately at the water. Hi Fella drank too, making more noise. After that they went on, past the cows, to a place where the grass was all flattened down, as if the cat had lain there often. In the middle of this patch it sat down and suddenly rolled on its back, wriggling and flipping from side to side, as though the dry grass gave it great pleasure. It flicked a paw at Hi Fella, making him wince and draw back. Then it lay stretched out, staring at him.

After a while the grasshoppers started coming back. One settled on a stalk quite close to them, and in a lightning move the cat seized it. For a moment the grasshoppper was held squirming between two forepaws. Then it was allowed to escape, and with lazy interest the cat watched it sail away.

They stayed in this place until the sun was over on the other side of the sky, shining between the two buildings. Then the cat moved again. Slipping to the very edge of the clearing, half hiding behind the trunk of a tree, it stared at the buildings.

17

Three people came out of the house on the left. Hi Fella started to run, but the cat seemed to have no fear of the people. With calm interest it watched their comings and goings, as if waiting for something. Yet it was careful to slip entirely behind the tree whenever one of the people glanced in their direction.

Finally a man walked toward the meadow, opened a gate, and called out.

"Hooey! Hooey! Hooey!"

That aroused the cows. Clumsily they got to their feet and lumbered toward the man, who led them through the gate and to the big building on the right. At the same time the other people carried armfuls of wood back into the house.

Now the clearing was empty again, but still the cat did not move.

The sun was a great fiery ball just above the horizon. Slowly it slipped down and down until it was no more than a sliver that spread bright red light over the ground. Then it was gone. The cows reappeared. Filing out of the building, with the man following, they returned to the meadow and at once started grazing again. The man closed the gate, walked across the clearing, and went into the house.

That seemed to be a signal for the cat.

Padding over to the gate, it slipped through the bars. Hi Fella tried to follow, but again his body was too big. Half in and half out of the gate he was stuck, unable to move one way or the other. Meanwhile the cat was circling toward the entrance of the big building.

With a wrench that tore out chunks of his fur, he finally managed to squeeze the rest of the way through the gate. In a mad dash he crossed the dangerous clearing. And all at once his fear was gone. The big building was a barn, very much like the one he had lived in once. It even smelled the same. He looked around, thinking he might see his mother, but there was only a black cat in a far corner, lapping milk out of a pan.

In a way, that made him feel even more at home. This cat was like the one back at the farm. It was small and slender, and it had a tail.

When the small cat caught sight of the bigger cat, it hastily thrust its tongue in and out a few more times, then backed off, and the bigger one took its place. The same thing must have happened many times before, because the little cat seemed to know it should go away, while the big one acted as if it owned the pan.

The milk smelled wonderful. Squatting nearby, the black cat did not growl or hiss at Hi Fella, but only stared. So he went to the pan and lowered his head, and winced, expecting the big cat to lash out at him. It did not, but while he drank he took care to stay on the opposite side, and as soon as the cat circled around to lick the pan clean, he moved out of the way.

Finally the big cat turned, and the little one went to sniff at the empty pan. But only a glance from the other one sent it scampering off through the barn door. The big one carefully washed its face, and after that it wandered around, jumping up on hayracks and down again, sniffing here and there, until everything was dark outside. Then it went into the clearing and sat quietly behind a pile of wood.

Light shone through the windows of the house. Hi Fella could hear people talking and moving around inside. Finally the door opened and a woman came out. She was carrying a plate.

At once the black cat ran to her and stood on its hind legs, begging for what was on the plate. As soon as the woman put the plate down it started eating.

The big cat waited until the woman had gone back into the house, then slipped across the clearing to the plate. This time the black cat did not back off but only edged away to keep distance between them. As the two cats ate, Hi Fella dashed in, grabbed a mouthful, and ran. Once that was down he came back for more, and stayed.

Soon the plate was empty. The black cat circled around to wash it and the big cat slipped away so swiftly that Hi Fella was almost left behind. Traveling next to the wire fence, they went to a place where water trickled down through rocks to make a small pool. Here they drank. And after that the cat headed for the cave.

Hi Fella listened while it rustled around inside the cave, and as soon as it was quiet he settled down outside, with his nose poked through the entrance.

The day had been good. He had enjoyed the lazy afternoon in the meadow, and he had had almost enough to eat. The cat was nicer to be with than the restless, grumpy raccoon, because it lived on the ground instead of up in a tree, and it slept when he liked to sleep, at night instead of during the day. It was also friendlier, in an offhand way.

Until almost dawn he slept well. Then he dreamed he was on the bank of the stream and the raccoon was jumping up and down, splashing water over him. The next moment he woke and discovered he really was being splashed, but not by the raccoon. It was raining. He was already soaking wet.

He got up and shook himself and looked with longing into the cave. The cat was breathing heavily, making little snoring sounds. Cautiously he stuck his head through the entrance. Nothing happened, and he eased in a bit more.

The cat was curled up on a pile of leaves at the far end of the cave, where it was narrowest. The smell of another animal was quite strong, as if someone else had lived here before the cat, and perhaps had made the bed of leaves on which it lay.

He moved in still more, until his rump was out of the rain. Then he noticed one of the cat's eyes was open, looking at him. Very slowly he sat down, watching the eye for any change of expression. After a while he slid one leg forward. When that seemed all right he did the same with the other leg, and gradually his body sank until he was lying down. Still the cat's eye stared at him. He put his head on his paws and stared back, and slowly the cat's eye closed.

What he really wanted was to get up and give himself a good shake, but he did not dare. At least he was out of the rain. The cave was dry and warm, a good comfortable place to be on such a miserable day. He wormed a little closer to the bed of the cat and watched warily as its legs twitched, as if it might be running in its sleep. Then it stretched and curled up tighter and put its paws over its eyes.

He liked the cat. He liked the cave. He curled up too, and soon he was sound asleep.

18

When he woke the cat was sitting up, washing drops of rain off its fur. It must have been outside, but not for long. Once it was satisfied every trace of water was gone, it squatted down to stare through the entrance of the cave, at the curtain of rain beyond.

Moving very carefully, Hi Fella went outside, lowering his head against the pelting rain. He did not stay long either. Before going back in he took care to shake himself, and he walked in slowly, staying close to the wall, as far from the cat as possible. It shifted around to tuck its forepaws under its chest, and continued to look out at the gloomy day.

Hi Fella's stomach rumbled. The sound made the cat's head jerk. It gave him a quick look and just as quickly looked away again, as if it understood he had not meant to make the noise.

Finally what light there was outside began to fade. The downpour was as heavy as ever, but suddenly the cat got up and ducked into the rain. When it did not come back Hi Fella went out and saw it was already some distance away, going through the woods in the direction of the clearing. He did not catch up until it stopped at a big puddle to drink. He drank too. Then they skirted the puddle and went on.

At the edge of the clearing they were just in time to watch the cows coming out of the barn. The cows did not seem to like the rain either. The man had to chase them and shout at them, until all three were in the meadow and he could close the gate.

His boots made a sucking noise as he slopped through the mud toward the house. The cat waited until he had closed the door, then led the way to the barn, where they found everything the same as the day before: the pan of milk in the corner, the little black cat lapping nervously and leaving as they approached.

The barn was dry and pleasant. Hi Fella hated to leave, but when they heard the woman come out of the house and go back in again, he was even faster than the cat in running to the plate.

There was not nearly enough to eat. The plate was empty in no time, and Hi Fella was still very hungry. When the cat squeezed through the gate to get into the meadow, he remembered the rabbit it had caught the day before, but also he remembered what a lot of trouble he had had with the gate. So he ran all the way around to his hole next to the big rock, then ran here and there through the wet grass hunting for the cat.

With his mind on nothing but getting his share of a rabbit, he was taken completely unawares when a dark shape rose before him, gave a great snort, and lunged sideways. It scared him so that he yelped. But again it was only a cow that he had startled. Easing past it and warily avoiding the other two, he snuffled around until he found the trail of the cat, and once more he was careless.

He approached from the rear, and much too fast. With a fierce snarl the cat jumped straight up into the air, twisting as it did so to face him. Its fur bristled. Its back arched. On stiff legs it stalked toward him, snorting with rage. Hi Fella braced himself for the attack, but gradually the cat seemed to recognize him. In the end all it did was hiss. Then it snatched up the mouse it had caught and moved a little away.

It chewed slowly, glancing up at him and growling every once in a while. Finally it licked both sides of its mouth, shook a paw and licked that, and walked off toward the pond.

Hi Fella smelled around the place where the cat had crouched, but there was nothing left of the mouse. For a moment he thought of going back to the house to see if any more food had been put on the plate, or to the barn to see whether more milk was in the pan. He especially liked the idea of the barn. It would be pleasant to lie there on the hay. But he trotted the other way, toward the pond.

The cat had left. He drank hastily, followed the trail to the fence, found and crawled through his hole, and went to the cave.

This time he walked boldly in. The cat gave him only a glance and went on washing. Settling down as close to its bed as he dared, he worked on pulling a burr from one of his paws, until the steady drumming of the rain outside made him drowsy. The soft rasping of the cat's tongue passing over its fur was a soothing sound. He gave up on the burr and closed his eyes.

Some time later he woke up feeling wonderfully

comfortable. His coat had dried, but that was not the only reason. Something pleasantly soft and warm was snuggled against him. Carefully he raised and turned his head, to discover the cat lying curled up between his legs.

Roused from sleep by his movement, it stretched and yawned. Then it thrust its forepaws into his fur to knead gently, while from its throat came a low, contented rumbling.

A small whimper escaped from his own throat.

On this day he had not had nearly enough to eat. But he had a fine home, and a good friend, and he was happy.

19

Except when it rained, the cat kept to about the same hours, going abroad around dawn and sleeping in the cave at night. But in other ways it was much less reliable than the raccoon, who had usually followed the same paths.

Most often the cat led the way to the meadow, where in the early morning rabbits were feeding and easier to catch. But sometimes it turned the other way, going to the woods where they had first met. Or sometimes it would have no luck in the meadow, and would go to hunt near the stream.

Hi Fella liked the meadow better. It was sunny and peaceful, and once he got used to the cows he rather liked being near them. But wherever the cat decided to go, he went along.

Scattered through the woods near the stream were many burrows where strange animals lived. Some were as big as the cat. Others were smaller. All were round and fat, so that they waddled when they walked. Yet if they were frightened they could dart over the ground in an amazing burst of speed.

If one was taken by surprise it gave a piercing whistle and dove into a burrow, only to pop its head out a moment later to have another look around. Once in a while the cat managed to pounce on a foolish little one that had strayed too far from a burrow, but the really big ones were left alone. When Hi Fella decided to try his luck, he encountered such a fierce snarling and snapping that he quickly changed his mind.

Just beyond the burrows the ground sloped gently, and down at the foot of the hill a part of the stream flowed into a wide marsh. Here other strange animals lived, in houses of roots and sticks that rose right out of the water. These animals were smaller than the cat but not easily caught, because they were very good swimmers. At the slightest hint of danger they dove into the water with a great splash, and only when they had gone some distance underwater did their heads appear again.

Both the animals who lived on the hill and those that lived in the water, as well as many others from the surrounding woods, came to the marsh to feed. It was a fine place to hunt. Usually the cat caught something almost at once. If the catch was fairly big, a portion might be left for Hi Fella. Otherwise he had to go hungry until evening, and be satisfied with whatever milk he could lap up in a hurry and whatever he could snatch from the plate.

He was no good at hunting. The cat crept forward slowly and silently, and pounced before the prey was aware of its presence. He just ran, giving the animal warning so that it had plenty of time to get away.

Once he did catch a mouse, but just held it in his mouth, thinking he ought to give it to somebody. So when the cat nosed in he dropped the mouse, and the cat snatched it up.

Although the marsh was such a good place to hunt, both he and the cat were uneasy there. Among all the other scents was one that they feared. Hi Fella was used to the man smell around the barn. That belonged there, along with the smell of the cows and the hay and the milk. But the man smell in the marsh was different. It recalled a terrifying memory, of a man holding a stick that exploded.

Sometimes they came across human footprints in the soft mud at the edge of the stream. The cat would stop to sniff at them, and from then on it would move with great caution, stopping often to listen and look around. It, too, seemed to know there was a difference between the smell of the people who came here and those who lived in the clearing.

20

One day when they visited the marsh they actually saw a man.

First they had gone to the meadow, but the rabbit the cat had stalked so carefully had glanced up at the last moment and escaped.

In its terror the rabbit had failed to notice Hi Fella, and leaped right in front of his nose. He made a grab for it and missed, as usual, but it had been so close that he was sure he could catch it. So he ran, zigzag-

93

ging all over the meadow as the rabbit kept changing course, until they came upon the stone wall. There the rabbit vanished.

When he got back to where he had left the cat, it was already leaving. His wild chase had surely driven off all the other game in the meadow.

That was why they went to the marsh on that day. As they came close, the cat stopped often to look about and crept forward with its body close to the ground. Hi Fella also tried to be as careful as possible. The man smell was very strong.

Then they saw him, sitting on a rock in front of one of the burrows. On his lap was one of the dreaded guns, pointed directly at the burrow.

Hi Fella backed up to hide behind a clump of bushes, but the cat seemed curious. In a wide circle it stalked around the man, keeping well out of sight in the brush, putting each paw down so carefully that it made not a sound. When it returned to Hi Fella a ridge of fur stood up all along its back and he could smell its fear.

The man sat without moving, staring at the burrow. Finally a small head poked out, and at once withdrew. Ever so slowly the man raised the gun. Nothing happened for a while. Then the head appeared again, and all at once the animal shot out of the burrow, heading in a great burst of speed for the marsh. And at that instant the gun exploded. With a horrible scream the animal leaped up in the air, and fell whimpering on the ground.

The man got up, went over to the twitching body, picked it up, and got rid of it by stuffing it back into the burrow. Then he glanced around and walked straight to where Hi Fella and the cat were hiding.

The cat flattened down, trying to make itself invisible. But as the man came closer still it suddenly went crazy. With a snarl of rage it shot out of the bushes to go leaping wildly through the woods. In a whirl of madness Hi Fella plunged after it, but all at once the cat stopped almost in the middle of a bound and went hurtling off in another direction. A moment later Hi Fella saw why. It had nearly run into another man walking over to join the first.

Exactly what happened after that was lost in terror and confusion. Hi Fella did not know where the cat was. He did not even know where he was. As he darted around trees and fought through brush he heard two explosions, and a terrifying whine passed swiftly over his head. Then the two men were shouting to each other.

"What was that? A bear cub?"

"Gee, what I saw looked like a bobcat."

"Did you hit it?"

"Gee, I don't know."

Heavy boots came tramping over the ground. Hi Fella paused only long enough to get his bearings. Then he veered to the right and raced for the cave.

All he thought about was getting safely inside the cave. As soon as he reached it he dove in, only to be greeted by snarls of rage and a furious slashing of claws. The cat had got there ahead of him and in its terror mistook him for an enemy.

He could not go outside again to face the men, and there was no place else to go. With his head bowed he just stood there taking the beating, until the cat calmed down and recognized him.

Turning away, it went back to sit on its bed of leaves and began washing nervously. Hi Fella huddled near the entrance, not daring to move one way or the other. Then they heard footsteps coming toward the cave, closer, and closer. The cat stopped washing and stood up, every muscle tensed to spring. Hi Fella pressed his body against the wall of the cave.

The feet were just outside. The man smell was strong, and so was the sharp odor of their guns. But the feet walked on, and away. Neither man had noticed that the rock was split, or how the earth in front of it had been trampled smooth, or even the small tuft of Hi Fella's fur caught on a snag near the entrance.

The cat settled down with its paws tucked under its chest. Hi Fella stayed just as he was for quite a long time. The cat's eyes stared steadily through the entrance, but finally, slowly, they closed.

Then Hi Fella stopped trembling and relaxed. Lying down, he stretched out his neck full length, so that his nose almost touched one side of the cat's lowered head.

21

After that they stayed away from the marsh. Each morning the cat turned the other way, toward the meadow. Sometimes it caught a rabbit there, sometimes it did not.

Near the stone wall where they liked to spend the afternoon, many nuts dropped from the big tree and lay all over the ground. Chipmunks and mice scurried around stuffing their mouths, taking the nuts to their burrows, and while they were so busy they were easy to catch. The cat caught so many that it became quite finicky, eating only the forepart and leaving the rest for Hi Fella.

These were good days in which he always had enough to eat. But finally the nuts were gone, and with them most of the mice and chipmunks. The few the cat did catch it ate entirely, and Hi Fella had to go hungry until they visited the barn and the house. But there he made up for lost time. His bigger tongue could lap up more milk, and at the plate he gulped down food much faster than the cats, who had to carefully chew each mouthful.

When they returned to the cave he was usually still hungry. Yet he was not actually starving. And he was glad to stay away from the marsh. Ever since they had been going to the meadow instead, life had been peaceful and without fear.

Then something happened to bring an end to the peace.

First of all, one of the cows did not go to the meadow with the others but stayed in the barn. She was shut up, so she could not really bother them while they were drinking the milk. But she made such a commotion, snorting and stamping and hooking her horns on the bars of her stall, that they were both nervous. The cat lapped and growled at the same time, and as soon as the milk was gone it went out of the barn to hide behind the woodpile.

After a while the woman came out of the house and put the plate down as usual, and everything seemed all right. Once she went back into the house she never came out again. The door always stayed closed. But on this night, just as they were starting to eat, it suddenly opened again.

The cat shot off in one direction, Hi Fella in another. Even the little black cat ran.

The boy who came out had a very bright light in his hand. He played it around the clearing, then went to the barn, where he stayed for a short time, and after that he walked here and there, shining the light in back of the barn, behind the woodpile, even along the sides of the house. At last he turned off the light and called through the open door.

"The cow's better, Dad. I think she can go out again tomorrow. Listen, Dad, I saw a couple of strange animals out here. It sounds crazy, but one looked like a bobcat, and the other one something like a bear cub. You think we ought to check on the other cows and make sure they're all right?"

"I don't think so. If anything bothered them we'd hear a ruckus. Your eyes can play tricks on you at night, son. Everything looks bigger than it really is. What you probably saw was just a couple of possums."

"It couldn't have been. Well, I'll wait a few minutes. Maybe they'll come back, and I can get a better look."

The boy went inside and the door closed, and the clearing was once more dark and quiet. Hi Fella started toward the plate, but before he was anywhere near it the door burst open again.

This time the bright light flashed on immediately, to reveal just the black cat eating at the plate. The light stayed on only a moment, and the door stayed open only a moment, but for quite a while Hi Fella was afraid to go near the plate, and when he finally did, it was empty.

That night, after he and the cat had returned to the cave, he was so hungry that he could not sleep. And from then on it was like that. It seemed he would never again get enough to eat.

22

Rabbits became scarce. Soon there were none at all in the meadow, except for the one that Hi Fella found. It was huddled up against the stone wall, and it was dead.

He picked it up and put it down again. The cat came over to sniff, then with the sweep of a paw raked sod over the carcass.

Hi Fella did not want it either, for it smelled of sickness. Yet he carried it around for quite a while, thinking he ought to give it to someone. Finally he put it down in front of one of the cows, and felt relieved. It had been an unpleasant burden he was glad to get rid of.

The day was cold and gloomy. Although the cat searched everywhere it found nothing to eat. Then when they went to the house after dark and the door opened, the woman did not appear. Instead, the boy came out and put down the plate. This was so strange that even the black cat stayed away.

But what was on the plate smelled wonderful. Once the door was closed, Hi Fella could not resist. He was first to get to the plate. The cat followed him. And a moment later the black one slipped out of the shadows. So they were all turned about on this night.

The plate was a different one, bigger, and piled high with food ground so fine that even the cats did not have to stop to chew. They gulped down morsels almost as fast as Hi Fella, until all three of them had to stop and run.

The big cat was the first to bolt when they heard the footsteps behind the door, but Hi Fella was not far behind. When the door opened and the bright light flashed on the plate, only the black cat stood blinking in the glare.

Someone inside the house spoke.

"Well, what did you see?"

"Nothing but our own cat. But a lot of the food is gone. She couldn't have eaten all that."

"You're just wasting money, putting out that expensive canned stuff. Whatever is out there, if there's anything at all, probably isn't worth it."

The door closed, and this time all three of them were back at the plate almost immediately. Even the big cat could not resist such fine food. Yet it kept glancing up and listening for any small sound that might mean the door was about to open again.

It did not again on that night, but the nights that followed were impossible. Time after time they heard footsteps and had to run. All three of them became short-tempered. The big cat growled at the little one. The little one edged away and bumped into Hi Fella. He snapped, and the little cat hissed. The big cat snarled at both of them. Then they heard a noise at the door, and once more they had to run.

Finally one evening they went to the barn as usual, but when the milk was gone the cat did not linger. Trotting around the side of the barn, it headed for the woods.

Hi Fella started to follow, thought of the good food that would be on the plate, and could not make up his mind what to do. He looked toward the house, looked toward the departing cat, and toward the house again. He sat down, and got up, and went to crouch behind the woodpile.

Being alone was strange. Several times he started to leave, only to turn around and sit down again. Once he brushed against the woodpile and a loose chunk came clattering down. It scared him so that he ran. Then he crept back, because the boy had come out of the house, and even at that distance he could smell the food on the plate.

Crossing the clearing without the cat made him uneasy. But as soon as he reached the plate everything else was forgotten. Slipping out of the shadows, the black cat came to join him, eating daintily on one side of the plate while he gulped down big mouthfuls on the other.

Always the big cat had given them warning when the door of the house was about to open. With his mind on the food he neglected to listen, so that when the boy came out he was taken completely by surprise. For a second the bright light shone directly on him. Then he was streaking away, across the clearing, past the barn, through the woods.

No rocks were thrown. No gun exploded. Yet fear pushed him all the way to the cave, where he sank down in a trembling heap.

23

The cat was not in the cave. Nor was it anywhere around outside. He whined, and the sound only made him feel more lonely.

At last he went back toward the clearing. Halfway there he came upon a fresh trail, which led him through the woods, into the brush, past the burrows, and down the hill to the marsh.

He was so preoccupied with tracking that he did not notice what a lot of noise he was making. Dry leaves rustled under his paws. Dead branches rattled as he passed by. And because he was nosing along with his head down, he did not see the cat until he was almost upon it.

Crouched near the edge of the marsh, it was staring at a young animal that had just crawled out of the water. Ever so slightly its rump began to wriggle, preparing for the capturing leap. And just at that moment Hi Fella stepped on a dry twig.

The snapping sound made the cat's head jerk around. For only a second it glanced away, but that gave the young animal time to dodge. With an angry snarl the cat pounced anyway and missed, pounced again and missed. Then there was a loud splash as the young animal dove into the water.

The cat growled so furiously that Hi Fella was afraid to move. Still growling, it stalked along the edge of the marsh, searching for other game, until suddenly it wheeled around.

Over to the right, some distance away, there had been a muffled click, followed by a violent thrashing. That suggested another animal might be in some kind of trouble and would be easy prey. At once the cat went bounding toward the sound, with Hi Fella not far behind.

When they were halfway there the thrashing stopped. Then Hi Fella heard another click, and something went wrong with the cat. Hissing savagely, it leaped straight up in the air, only to be jerked back. As Hi Fella watched in terror it leaped again, was pulled back again, and fell writhing on the ground.

Fighting off some enemy that Hi Fella could not see, the cat twisted and turned and doubled up, snapping at one of its hind legs. But whatever had seized it there hung on. Rolling over on its back, the cat let out a piercing scream. Then it lay still, panting and moaning softly. Warily Hi Fella went closer. Jaws of some kind had snapped shut on the cat's leg, high up, near the body. From these jaws a short chain was drawn tight over to a stake driven into the ground.

He tried his teeth on the chain. The metal was very hard. The cat lifted its head to look at him, and mewed so sadly that he whimpered. Then it began flinging its body around again, and he had to back away. This time the terrible thrashing did not last so long. Once more the cat lay gasping. Then it doubled up, sniffed at the leg, and started chewing where the jaws bits into the flesh.

While it worked its breath came in short, sharp rasps. It cried out in pain, licked away the blood and nosed against the wound, and turned its head away. The jaws were too high up. The entire leg could not be chewed off.

For a while it seemed to sleep. Then suddenly it was fighting again, clawing the earth, trying to drag the stake out of the ground. Once more it wailed, and was quiet. Hi Fella pawed at the stake, but it had been driven deep between two rocks.

Now the cat lay very still. When Hi Fella went close it did not move. He shoved with his nose, and the limp body fell back in the same position. Pacing around and around, he started to whine.

The sky in the east lightened, and he was so tired that he seemed to be dreaming. Everything was mixed up. The cat was the raccoon, and the time had come for them to return to the den tree. Slowly he trotted toward the cave, and, once there, hurried back again, to speak to the cat in desperate whimpers.

There was no response. For quite a long time he stared at the motionless body. In a way he could not understand, the cat had left him. He barked to bring it back, and when that did no good he howled.

The sound was comforting. Having begun, he could not stop. Raising his head, he howled and howled at the rising sun.

24

He very nearly missed hearing the footsteps, not too far away on the hill, coming directly toward him. At once he stopped howling and looked at the cat, expecting it to get up and run. Instinct told him to head for the cave while there was still time, but he could not leave the cat, and it did not move. Slowly he backed away and hid in the nearby brush.

Then he saw them. One was the boy who had been bringing out the plate of food each night. The other was the man who always came for the cows in the meadow. The boy started calling.

"Dog? Come on, dog. Where are you? It must be around here somewhere.... Careful, Dad. Watch your step. This hill is full of woodchuck burrows. Hey, look, Dad! What's that?"

"Oh, my!"

The two people had seen the cat. They hurried over and knelt beside it. The man touched the body, felt the jaws, pried them apart, and eased out the leg.

"Is it dead?"

"I think—no, it's still breathing. Just barely. Lost quite a bit of blood. See here, how it tried to chew its leg to get free?"

"Gee. What is it, a bobcat?"

"Looks something like one, but it isn't. It's a Manx. Used to be a lot of wild Manx in the woods around here, but hunters kept mistaking them for bobcats. They're pretty scarce now."

"Dad, this trap isn't even legal. There's no name on it."

"Not legal anyway. This is our land, and we gave no one permission to trap on it."

"Well, then—"

The boy kicked at the stake, kicked and kicked until it was loosened. Then he pulled it up, swung the trap on the chain, and let go. Stake, chain, and trap went through the air, splashed in the marsh water, and sank.

The man had taken off his jacket and spread it on the ground. Carefully he slid the cat's body onto the jacket and picked it up.

From his hiding place in the brush Hi Fella watched the two people walking away, the man with the cat cradled in his arms. After they had gone some distance he started following, keeping into the brush, putting each paw down carefully, so as to make no noise. But suddenly, with one paw lifted to take another step, he had to stop because the people had stopped.

"Look there, son."

"Another trap! That's a muskrat in it. Good and dead."

"Well, take it out and hide it so the trapper won't find it, and get rid of the trap. As soon as this cat is taken care of, we'll come back and see if there are any more."

The boy put the dead muskrat in a clump of bushes and covered it with leaves. Then he kicked out the stake and flung the second trap into the water.

The two people started walking again, the man still holding the cat. Cautiously Hi Fella started following again, stopping each time the boy looked over his shoulder.

"I have the funniest feeling something's coming along behind us, Dad. You know, we did hear a dog howling. That was why we came out here. Maybe it's following us."

"The dog we heard could be half a mile away by this time. But when we go back to check for traps we can look around."

The people were heading toward the clearing. Hi Fella veered over to the right, making a detour to the safe spot at the edge of the woods, where he and the cat always went for a good view of the barn and the house and any activity in the clearing.

He arrived just in time to see the man and the boy go into the barn. For quite a while after that nothing happened. Then the two people came out again, and the man no longer had the cat in his arms. Hi Fella watched them cross the clearing and go into the house, and when the door was closed he crept toward the barn.

The time of day was wrong. Yet he thought he might find the pan in the corner, and the cat squatting there lapping the milk. That was the first thing he looked for. But there was no pan, and no sign of the cat.

Raising his head, he paced around, sniffing the air. At the far end of the barn the scent of the cat was stronger. Wire stopped him. But on the other side of the wire, half hidden in a mound of hay, there was a gleam of fur.

He whimpered. There was no answer. Snuffling along the wire, he searched for a way to get through. When he found none he started clawing at the wire, making such a noise that he did not hear the people coming back until almost too late.

In a wild dash he tried to escape through the doorway, only to run headlong into a pair of legs. With a yelp he shied away from them, and crashed into the door. That sent him sprawling, but he managed to scramble back onto his feet. Then he bolted, across the clearing, into the woods.

No gun exploded. All he heard was someone calling out to him.

"Here, dog! Come on, we won't hurt you. Hi there, fella!"

Hi Fella was his name. He stopped to look around, and in a rush many memories of the past came to him. He thought of his mother, and the farmer, and the barn where he had lived, and the food the farmer had always put down near the steps. Slowly he turned and walked back to stand at the edge of the woods.

The man and the boy were just outside the barn. He stared at them, looked toward the woods, and looked at them again. Then he sat down.

"Hi, fella. Don't be afraid."

The voice sounded kind, but he was not sure. Once more he glanced toward the woods. But he did not move.

"We'd better get this milk and whiskey into the cat while it's still warm. Come on, I don't think he'll go away."

Once the people were inside the barn, Hi Fella knew he should escape while he still could. But all at once he was very, very tired. The sun was warm on his fur. The clearing was peaceful. Nothing stirred anywhere, except a fly that kept buzzing around his ears.

He shook his head to get rid of the fly, then shook his whole body to get rid of the sleepiness.

He could go back to the cave and wait for the cat. Or he could go to the stone wall at the far end of the meadow, where the cat liked to sun itself on a lazy day like this. Instead he just sat down and stared at the barn.

Footsteps jerked him from a doze. The man and the boy were coming out of the barn. He half got up to run, changed his mind, and crouched down, thinking they might not notice him.

"He's still there."

"Yeah. Hi, fella! Come on, there's a good dog."

Good Dog was another of his names. The farmer had always called him that when he was pleased. Maybe now the man was pleased. He remembered how he had always bounded around the farmer's feet when he was called Good Dog, and slowly his tail swept over the ground.

"Your friend is awake. Took a bit of milk too. Here, would you like some milk?"

The pan was the one that just before dark he and the cat always found on the floor of the barn. The man held it out, and he could smell the milk.

He would go and drink a little of it. Then he would run.

The man put the pan on the ground and knelt beside it, with his hand on the rim. Hi Fella took a step toward it, and another step, and another. Then he was at the pan, lapping the milk, thinking of nothing else. Not until the pan was empty and licked clean did he notice how close the man's hand was. Cautiously he sniffed at it.

The hand smelled of hay and earth and the barn and the cows, like another hand he had known and trusted. The cat's scent was on it too. As he sniffed, it turned over, very slowly, to let him touch his nose against the palm, and this was a gesture he under-

118

stood. In such a position the hand did not threaten. It offered friendship.

"Good dog."

The hand was raised to gently stroke his head.

"Come on, fella."

The man and the boy went back into the barn, and he followed. Just in front of the pen in which the cat lay there was now another mound of hay. He went to it and stood looking through the wire at the cat. The cat looked at him, and lifted its head a little, and opened its mouth in a silent mew.

The hay rustled as the tip of Hi Fella's tail quivered. The sound was soothing, reminding him of home. He pressed his body against the wire that separated him from the cat, sank down on the hay, and sighed.

The man spoke softly. "There, now."

When the man and the boy were gone, the barn was very quiet. Pushing his nose through the wire as far as it would go, Hi Fella gazed at the cat, and the cat gazed at him. Finally the cat's eyes closed, and from its throat came a small, contented rumble. Hi Fella opened his mouth in a satisfied yawn. Then he shifted to a more comfortable position on his bed of hay, and put his head down on his paws.

Now everything was all right. After a long, long time, he was home again.

120

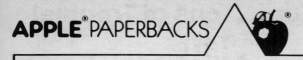
APPLE® PAPERBACKS

More books you'll love, filled with mystery, adventure, friendship, and fun!

NEW APPLE TITLES

☐ 40388-5	**Cassie Bowen Takes Witch Lessons** Anna Grossnickle Hines		$2.50
☐ 33824-2	**Darci and the Dance Contest**	Martha Tolles	$2.50
☐ 40494-6	**The Little Gymnast**	Sheila Haigh	$2.50
☐ 40403-2	**A Secret Friend**	Marilyn Sachs	$2.50
☐ 40402-4	**The Truth About Mary Rose**	Marilyn Sachs	$2.50
☐ 40405-9	**Veronica Ganz**	Marilyn Sachs	$2.50

BEST-SELLING APPLE TITLES

☐ 33662-2	**Dede Takes Charge!**	Johanna Hurwitz	$2.50
☐ 41042-3	**The Dollhouse Murders**	Betty Ren Wright	$2.50
☐ 40755-4	**Ghosts Beneath Our Feet**	Betty Ren Wright	$2.50
☐ 40950-6	**The Girl With the Silver Eyes**	Willo Davis Roberts	$2.50
☐ 40605-1	**Help! I'm a Prisoner in the Library**	Eth Clifford	$2.50
☐ 40724-4	**Katie's Baby-sitting Job**	Martha Tolles	$2.50
☐ 40725-2	**Nothing's Fair in Fifth Grade**	Barthe DeClements	$2.50
☐ 40382-6	**Oh Honestly, Angela!**	Nancy K. Robinson	$2.50
☐ 33894-3	**The Secret of NIMH**	Robert C. O'Brien	$2.25
☐ 40180-7	**Sixth Grade Can Really Kill You**	Barthe DeClements	$2.50
☐ 40874-7	**Stage Fright**	Ann M. Martin	$2.50
☐ 40305-2	**Veronica the Show-off**	Nancy K. Robinson	$2.50
☐ 41224-8	**Who's Reading Darci's Diary?**	Martha Tolles	$2.50
☐ 41119-5	**Yours Till Niagara Falls, Abby**	Jane O'Connor	$2.50

Available wherever you buy books...or use the coupon below.

Scholastic Inc. P.O. Box 7502, 2932 E. McCarty Street, Jefferson City, MO 65102

Please send me the books I have checked above. I am enclosing $_____
(please add $1.00 to cover shipping and handling). Send check or money order-no cash or C.O.D.'s please.

Name_____

Address_____

City_____ State/Zip_____

Please allow four to six weeks for delivery. Offer good in U.S.A. only. Sorry, mail order not available to residents of Canada. Prices subject to change.

APP987

Lots of Fun...Tons of Trouble!

by Ann M. Martin

Kristy, Claudia, Mary Anne, Stacey, and Dawn – they're the Baby-sitters Club!

The five girls at Stoneybrook Middle School get into all kinds of adventures...with school, boys, and, of course, baby-sitting!

Join the Club and join the fun!

PREFIX CODE 0-590-

Available wherever you buy books...or use the coupon below.

Scholastic Inc. P.O. Box 7502, 2932 E. McCarty Street. Jefferson City, MO 65102

Please send me the books I have checked above. I am enclosing $_____

(please add $1.00 to cover shipping and handling). Send check or money order – no cash or C.O.D.'s please.

Name_____

Address_____

City_____ State/Zip_____

Please allow four to six weeks for delivery. Offer good in U.S.A. only. Sorry, mail order not available to residents of Canada. Prices subject to change.